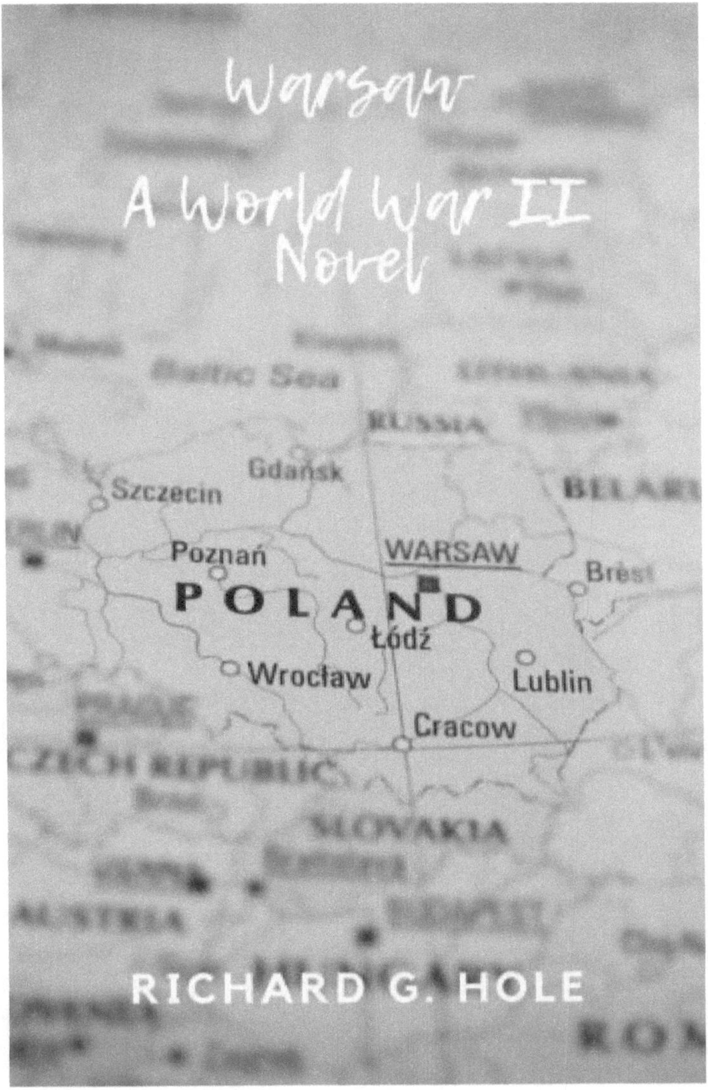
Warsaw
A World War II Novel
Baltic Sea
RUSSIA
Gdansk
Szczecin
Poznań
WARSAW
Brest
POLAND
Łódź
Wrocław
Lublin
Cracow
CZECH REPUBLIC
SLOVAKIA
RICHARD G. HOLE

Warsaw
A World War II Novel

1

Richard G. Hole

World War II

SYNOPSIS

The uprising, in Warsaw, of the Polish Clandestine Resistance Army was an act of arms that occurred in the Second World War, not without importance.

The proximity of the Russian troops gave the Poles hopes of success and they rose up in Warsaw, trusting in the arrival of Marshal Vatupin's soldiers.

For sixty-three days, Germans and Poles fought fiercely for possession of the city.

The fate of Warsaw continued to be played throughout history.

Warsaw is a story belonging to the World War II collection, a series of war novels developed in World War II

WARSAW

CHAPTER I

ON THE MARGINS OF WAR

It was cold. Aleska raised the collar of her summer coat and walked through the streets. People who passed her gave her a brief glance and continued on her way. It was beginning to get dark and the proximity of the war made that in that year of 1943 in the city of Warsaw everyone retired as soon as possible.

Aleska had finished her work at the offices of the Swiss Washing Machine Company where her services were, and was on her way to the appointment she had made.

With her they crossed several German soldiers, bored and disoriented, who were looking for a place to have fun. One of them stopped her and asked in broken Polish:

"Can't you tell us where we'll have dinner?

Aleska shrugged and continued on her way. From the river came a strong current of air and a mist rose that was spreading through the nearby streets.

When crossing one of the Vistula bridges, towards Stare Miasto of the population, he spotted a military column that was heading towards the station, with a rhythmic step, its head held high and singing proudly.

Aleska shuddered, huddling in her coat. Despite being the month of July, the nights were cool. The girl paid no attention to the people who were looking at her. She was twenty-seven and used to this happening. Tall, shapely and slender, her sporty and elegant figure attracted attention since she was very young. Her rosy face, with classic features, exerted a lively attraction on the men, who never ceased to praise her deep blue eyes, nor her lips, red and well drawn. Her blonde hair, of an old gold tone, was gathered in a bun, which had just given her a statuary air that her sincere and determined expression broke.

He crossed the bridges, heading for the appointment he had made. A gendarme beckoned to her, forcing her to stop. Armed soldiers and troops were seen in trucks.

Aleska showed her passport and the gendarme let her pass after greeting her. He overheard a citizen comment about a dead German soldier and a recent shooting. I don't pay much attention, feeling concerned only about the appointment she was going to and fearing that the incident would prevent her.

The old quarter of Warsaw, with its dark, narrow streets and dirty buildings, did not look pretty. But the girl went on quietly. At last he came to a deep and wide restaurant.

Aleska stepped into him, looking over at him. The person he was looking for did not seem to be there and he sat down at a table, ordering a cup of black tea. The clientele was made up almost exclusively of Poles, including some German uniforms.

The large counter, on which a huge coffeepot stood, was crowded with people.

Waiters, dressed in ancient costumes, paced from table to table, serving the clientele. Cigar smoke and the murmur of conversation made for a thick atmosphere.

Suddenly the door to the street opened and a young name, about twenty-three years old, dressed in a leather raincoat and covered with a floppy hat entered the premises, approaching the counter. Aleska barely looked at him, keeping an eye on her tea. The man glanced around the place and then leaned against the counter. He took a cigarette out of a pack and carefully lit it, waving the match in the air.

Seconds later, another man entered the restaurant. He was tall and strong, elegant-looking. He would be about thirty-two years old. She wore a leather coat, cinched at the waist, and had bare blonde hair. His distinguished features had a stamp of energy and audacity, veiled by a bitter and concentrated expression. His manly features would always have made him stand out as a handsome man. His clear pupils had a straight and firm gaze. His tanned complexion indicated a man accustomed to life in the open and something about him gave away the professional military man.

He approached the table where the girl was sitting. He smiled, holding out his hand.

Hello, Aleska.

She replied, twitching her red lips:

Hello, Stanislas.

The newcomer sat down at the table, ordering a drink. Sitting facing the door next to the girl, he kept his right hand buried in his coat pocket. The other man was at the counter, in the same position.

"Sorry if I'm late," Stanislas said, "but the police were demanding documentation.

Aleska nodded.

"I have seen them. I was afraid you would not come to the appointment.

The man smiled, gazing at her with poorly concealed tenderness.

"It would take many soldiers to prevent me from meeting you.

The girl played with her cigarette for a moment, then added:

"By God, Stanislas, don't expose yourself uselessly.

"Do you think seeing you is a useless thing?

Aleska looked down for a moment. He was slow to respond and finally exclaimed:

"Our friendship is wide and sincere enough for me to understand that one day it may be impossible for you to come.

"Friendship?

Stanislas's question was so direct that the girl did not know what to answer. Then he said again:

"After all, I am a foreigner.

The Pole nodded.

"Fortunately, you are a foreigner and, as a Swiss, you don't have to join either side. It is fortunate in times like this, for a woman, to be able to stay out of everything that happens.

Aleska shrugged.

"Anyway, I'm here and a friendship joins you.

"Friendship? Stanislas said again.

For the second time, she did not reply. Change of conversation, and looking at him fixedly, asked:

"When this is over, what do you plan to do?

He shrugged.

"First of all, I don't know if this will ever end and if I will be alive. But I can assure you that I no longer plan for the future. I believed that circumstances could not cut short my life. Captain Stychel of the Polish cavalry was sure of himself. Then the war broke out and I had to lead my spearmen against the German tanks. I never believed that circumstances would place me in this situation. No, I am not making plans. I live by the day and tomorrow Stanislas Stychel will do what the circumstances dictate.

Aleska hesitated for a moment.

"If you wanted, I could get you a means of getting out of Poland and going to Switzerland. There you could rebuild your life or march with Anders's troops.

He denied with his head.

"I follow my luck, without making plans. Today's reality prevails.

CHAPTER II

ON GUARD

The Komandatur building one of the largest and oldest buildings in Warsaw, it was surrounded by cars. The troops who stood guard outside the building appeared nervous and restless. There were too many category managers, capable of discovering an annoying detail on a soldier's uniform and charging him with a season of arrest. Like good veterans, they had guessed that this day was going to be annoying, and they polished their clothes and metal emblems until they gleamed. The well-oiled boots looked like a reception.

With their helmets held by the chinstrap, the soldiers remained motionless, rifles on their shoulders, while important figures entered and left.

A field car pulled up, driven by a sturdy soldier with a sun-and-snow-beaten face, bearing the emblems of the stormtroopers. The soldier jumped to the ground and opened the door. A tall, slender officer, with a distinguished air and irreproachable uniform, appeared, followed by another, younger and sporty-looking officer.

The first officer martially returned the driver's salute and headed toward the headquarters. His boots gleamed and the uniform was well cut and tailored to his athletic figure. On his shoulder pads he wore the emblems of a lieutenant colonel. The braided cap covered his blond hair and shadowed his weathered countenance with energetic and virile features. His jaw appeared aggressive and dominant. His gray pupils had a haughty, straight look. A scar ran from his temple to his chin, a memory of some combat. He was only thirty years old and commanded the shock battalion stationed in Warsaw. His name Peter von Ritcher, represented that of an old family of Prussian junkers, all military, and also that of a hero of all the campaigns carried out by the German army in that war. He had started the lieutenant war, but he soon distinguished himself and received medals and wounds. Promotions were swift, but his character did not change in the least, and just as Lieutenant von Ritcher had been one of the most cheerful and elegant officers in Berlin society, Lieutenant-Colonel von Ritcher was still on the field, preserving his well-groomed clothes and aristocratic mannerisms. The battalion he commanded would have followed him to hell, and there was no soldier who was not proud to obey him. Lieutenant Colonel von Ritcher was still on the field, preserving his well-groomed clothes and aristocratic manner. The battalion he commanded would have followed him to hell, and there was no soldier who was not proud to obey him. Lieutenant Colonel von Ritcher was still on the field, preserving his well-groomed clothes and aristocratic manner. The battalion he commanded would have followed him to hell, and there was no soldier who was not proud to obey him.

He was followed by his assistant captain, Schulz, twenty-three, who was only a cadet when the fighting broke out. But he had had a good run and he was satisfied.

A staff officer greeted Peter inside the building. Von Ritcher took off his cap and asked:

"Have they called me to notify me of the transfer?"

"No sir. This is an important meeting. The general awaits you.

Peter grimaced and entered a vast room, covered with city plans and in which the chiefs of all the garrison units had gathered. Ritcher squared himself before his general, a middle-aged man, straight and gruff. Once he was seated, while General Schellenberg prepared to speak, Peter surveyed the assembled colonels and lieutenant colonels. Next to the general was a portly officer with a sour face. It was Colonel Haller, Chief of Police. On the other side was a gray-faced, blank-eyed major, wearing the uniform of the General Staff.

It was Major Gentzel, head of the secret service, in charge of maintaining the cohort of spies, counter-spies, agents provocateurs and confidants, spread throughout Warsaw.

The general cleared his throat and began to say:

"The situation of the war on the eastern front is not the most promising for us. Russian troops are advancing on Poland and it is to be expected that as they get much closer to Warsaw, the situation here will become more difficult. The forces of the Clandestine Army will be ready to rise up the moment the Russians are far enough away to help them. We know that they have received a lot of material by plane and that there is great concern among the elements of the Clandestine Army. On the other hand, this restlessness is guessed in the environment. General Bor-Komorowski, the Polish leader, must prepare for an uprising. It is to be expected that attacks and acts of sabotage will increase.

"Our situation, so close to an approaching front, makes us the hub of communications. We must avoid, however, that sabotage and attacks can prevent the transport of troops, food or ammunition, from being interrupted. Watch tirelessly and have your strength ready for any event.

"In the event of an uprising, each one would be indicated a sector of the city, with the exception of Lieutenant Colonel von Ritcher, who would march with his unit towards the place of greatest danger or through which it was necessary to attack. But we will all leave the old part of the city, to retire towards the outskirts. Then we would charge on the population. We are not interested in leaving pockets of resistance that would reduce our numbers and result in useless sacrifices. "The general paused and then added," Major Gentzel will address you.

The inscrutable officer stood up and began to say:

"The agents and confidants we have among the Polish clandestine forces inform us that there is a lot of activity among them. Events are expected from one moment to the next and they have received numerous weapons. General Bor-Komorowski appears to be in Warsaw, but we have achieved nothing yet. We are also interested in locating a Polish colonel who is nicknamed "SS Colonel." These are the data that we have and that confirm that from one moment to another, depending on the events of the war, the rise of the clandestine troops will develop.

Major Gentzel was silent and the general said, closing the meeting:

"They will receive the orders they must follow in a timely manner. Three times a day, they will contact this Command, to warn them of any news. Good Morning.

The officers rose to their feet, preparing to depart. Ritcher approached the general, steadying himself. He smiled, holding out his hand.

"Hello, Peter" he said familiarly. Although I hardly dare to treat you with such confidence. You are quite a lieutenant colonel. Have you had a letter from your father?

"Yes, my general. He continues to command his army corps in Russia. I'd like to go back there, sir.

Schellenberg shook his head.

"I have seen your request, but I cannot attend to it, Warsaw, you have already heard it, it is of great importance to us. This is almost the front and I'm interested in having you here. You have specialized in blows and openings. You are a practical officer in dangerous operations and this here is going to be precisely the kind of war that you know. No, Peter, you are not in the rear.

Ritcher sighed.

"As ordered, my general. But I don't like being a cop.

Colonel Haller, who had overheard the conversation, exclaimed:

"Soon it will not be a matter of the police, Ritcher, but of the soldiers. Don't you notice something strange in the environment?

Peter nodded.

CHAPTER III

UNDER THE SHADOWS OF THE NIGHT

Warsaw rested under the overcast sky. The moon had hidden behind the clouds and a thick darkness hung over the town. In the distance, towards the Russian border, the roads of war stretched and at night the trains carrying troops whistled.

On the outskirts of Warsaw, out of the way followed by the patrols, lay a thick, dense forest. The paths forced us to march single file, or scattered through the trees. It was easy to ambush, but every now and then German troops would scramble for him, looking for partisans or fugitives.

Three men appeared lying on the ground, rifles at arm's length. Their civilian clothes gave them away as members of the Polish Clandestine Army.

The three men were silent, staring into the distance. A little further away, three others stood guard behind a thick oak.

The guard posts were being extended, so that they could sound the alarm before any danger.

In the forest loomed the outlines of a vast and gloomy edifice. It looked like an abandoned farmhouse. At the door, two men with submachine guns on their arms paced silently, watching for any sign of danger.

A large number of men were gathered inside the building. The room, lit by petroleum lanterns, appeared hermetically closed, without the glare of the illuminations filtering through a single opening.

The people who gathered there were of very different conditions. Some were older, tough-looking and determined, as if they were factory workers or peasants on the outskirts of Warsaw. Others looked like employees of different companies. One stood out for his elegant clothes and distinguished manner.

Over their coats and raincoats, they wore cartridge belts and on their shoulders they carried a rifle or a submachine gun.

Others were young and vigorous, and some, in considerable numbers, almost children. But they all had determined and energetic expressions.

In the center of the room were three men. One of them was Stanislas Stychel. To his right stood Noraczewski and to his left a hardened, gray-haired man. He was a former NCO from the Uhlans, a metalworker during the peace. It is called Dmowaki.

He announced, in a voice accustomed to commanding:

"Colonel S. S, is going to review them. Prepare yourselves.

Then he nodded toward his superior.

"Thank you, Major.

Stanislas approached the men and examined the weapons. With a natural gesture, they showed him the rifle or the submachine gun and then the equipment they possessed. Stychel was correcting the defects that he found or congratulating the man whose weapons were in order.

Dmowaki reprimanded company chiefs, according to the colonel's observations.

Stanislas, for some reason, was remembering the change in his life in those years. During Poland's short but mind-blowing campaign, he had met Petty Officer Dmowaki, a volunteer from the first hour. His drive and determination impressed him. Later, when the army was defeated and dispersed, when the organization of the clandestine troops began, which at first were only bands of desperate people or marauders, they managed to locate the non-commissioned officer again. Little by little, both were gaining in graduation and experience. Then Dmowaki was older and his second in command of that group of fighters.

The long-awaited hour of the uprising against the occupation troops seemed to be approaching. But there was only one cloud in Stanislas's soul. The uprising could have a bad outcome or it could be an adventure in which no one knew what it was exposing. What would become of Aleska?

He passed his hand over his forehead, to ward off those thoughts. Only duty should matter to him. The rest, he had nothing in common with them. They were members of an army and in their discipline they had to live.

After reviewing the troop, he stood in the center and surveyed his subordinates.

"Boys" he began to say, "you know, because you can see in the atmosphere that the Russian forces are advancing towards Poland. The heart of our homeland is Warsaw, and we are interested in occupying it ourselves before they do. Therefore, as they approach the Polish border, we will rise up in arms and occupy the capital. Then we will gather all the partisan forces of Poland, to form a new army. The hour is drawing near. Be prepared. During this time, acts of sabotage and attacks may increase. Almost all of you have experience in these matters, but you need to know it more thoroughly.

There was a long silence, and in a little while a lean man in a fur coat stepped forward.

"You speak, captain" invited Stychel.

"My colonel, we have rifles and light automatic weapons, which will be very useful for attacks and hand-to-hand combat. But in the event of an uprising, we will need heavy equipment and accompanying weapons. I suppose you have already thought about this, but I feel like it is my duty to say so.

Stanislas nodded.

"It is planned. This armament exists and everything is ready for distribution at the precise moment. Remember that you were made to learn its handling.

The captain bowed his head and replied:

"Thank you a thousand, my colonel.

Stychel went on to say:

"The Warsaw garrison is not made up, as long ago, of public order troops and police only. The German command, who knows their trade, has understood the difficult situation in which a Russian advance would place them and have reinforced it with front-line troops, including a seasoned and veteran shock battalion. This is the one that should concern us the most. They are men used to melee and surprise attacks. In a city, they would fight with the same advantage as us. On the other hand, their boss, Lieutenant Colonel von Ritcher, has a well-established reputation for being brave and daring. It seems that he teaches his troops to know the city in depth, so that nothing can fail them. We must be careful with that man. Try to recognize him right away.

Another officer stepped forward.

"How can we do it, my colonel?

"His name is Peter von Ritcher. It will be somewhat younger than me. Tall, strong and sporty. He is a serene man, who never alters the expression on his face. Try to go to witness the training of his troops or the changing of the guard. It is always there. Engrave his features in memory, for when the order is given to suppress him.

They all nodded silently. Through the minds of the men gathered there passed the image of themselves fighting in the middle of the street and fighting against the invaders.

Stanislas added:

"Now go back to your homes and be prepared.

CHAPTER IV

SENTIMENTAL INTERMEDIATE

On Sunday a summer sun shone.

The trees raised their green branches to the sky. Nothing seemed to indicate that the troops were fighting and killing each other far away. Only now and then was there a faraway, muffled murmur. They were the heavy caliber guns.

Stanislas and Aleska walked through the forest, looking at each other and laughing. They had decided to leave Warsaw that Sunday and go to rest in the country.

Aleska was smiling, looking at the panorama.

"It is very different from Switzerland," he said.

Stanislas nodded.

"Poland is unlike any of the lands that surround it. Perhaps only to the border areas of East Prussia and Russia. But it is different. It has something that also makes us different.

The girl nodded.

"And where are we going to eat?

"There is a hostel near here, where we will be fine.

Aleska hesitated for a moment.

"Wouldn't it be preferable to go eat in the country?

But he insisted.

"We will be better there.

They followed a moment in silence, as if she had been annoyed by the stubbornness of the young man. In a little while the girl smiled.

"I am convinced that we will be very well.

He nodded.

"Polish dishes will surely be strange to you, but they are very well seasoned there. And if you stay in Poland you must learn to like them.

Aleska laughed.

"Luckily, they are Swiss at the pension and we continue to eat at home.

The young man was silent for a moment.

"At home" he repeated.

Suddenly, a German motorized column was seen advancing down the road. The soldiers were singing, sitting in the vehicles. Stanislas contemplated them in silence and, biting the words, exclaimed:

"We will soon kick you out of Poland.

Aleska turned to him, surprised. Stychel smiled, as if to make him forget what he had said.

They were already at the parador, an old building nestled among some trees, not far from the road. The owner, a determined and smiling old woman, installed them at a table, preparing to serve them food. The waiter came soon.

Among the clientele were a couple of German officers and some soldiers chatting with some girls.

Stanislas was silent. They had a few glasses of liquor and then the food was served. The two young men laughed, talking animatedly, as if nothing was happening. But you could see in their attitudes that something had come between them. Both Stanislas and Aleska seemed concerned and nervous, partly oblivious to each other's company.

Suddenly, Stanislas proposed:

"Let's go for a walk, okay?

The two young men walked away from the inn, in silence. Stanislas lit a cigarette and gazed out at the verdant plain that stretched out in the distance. There were only meadows, meadows, and trees surrounding the houses. But his men and groups of partisans who harassed the German troops were hiding in them.

Then he turned to look at Warsaw. The roofs of the buildings rose to the sky. The well-known domes of St. John's Cathedral stood out above all others.

This was to be his battlefield.

He turned to the girl, realizing that she was looking at him. Those blue eyes touched her heart. He felt again the excitement he had experienced the first day he had seen Aleska.

She might have guessed what he was feeling, because she smiled, resting her hand on the young man's arm.

Stanislas took his hand and exclaimed:

"Aleska, I don't know what is going to happen.

"Because you said so?

He shrugged.

"War is an adventure and nobody knows how it will end.

After a brief pause, as if to emphasize the words well, the girl added:

"But you are not in the war. This one concluded for you.

He diverted the conversation.

"In Poland there is war and it is not easy to know what is going to happen. So there is one thing I would like you to know in case something happens.

Aleska raised her head, between curious and scared.

"What is it?

Stanislas shook the girl's hand tighter, and then said:

"Aleska, it is not difficult to realize what is happening to me. I've fallen in love with you.

Aleska fixed her blue pupils on him, full of tenderness.

"That is true?

"Yes, Aleska" he replied, approaching. I love you with all my soul.

The girl looked at him in silence, and then, raising her arms, murmured:

"Stanislas, my love.

They embraced passionately, while she rested her head on the young man's shoulder. Stychel kissed her cheeks, muttering:

"I would like to offer you the best in the world and I cannot say or think about the future.

The girl kissed him on the mouth, adding:

"Don't talk about the future. You are right. War is an uncertain adventure.

Together they returned to the inn. They remained seated at the table, looking into each other's eyes and smiling. Their hands were linked and everything was alien to them.

"Fortunately," the young man said again, "you belong to a neutral nation and none of this can affect you.

She affectionately rebuked him:

"We have decided not to talk about the future or current circumstances at all. Remember it.

The young man nodded and his pupils suddenly hardened. She instinctively followed Stychel's gaze. Noraczewski had arrived at the inn, in a small car. Smiling, he approached the table and greeted the two young men.

"What a coincidence to find you here" he said.

Stanislas nodded.

"How's it going?

"I have come to look for a cousin of mine and I return to; Warsaw. If you want, I'll take you with me.

Stychel nodded.

CHAPTER V

BEFORE REALITY

The orderly, at a signal from Major Gentzel, opened the door. The military man smiled slightly and stood up, holding out his hand.

"Sit down, miss.

Aleska bowed her thanks and obeyed. The secret service chief's office was dim. The street was still bustling with passersby and onlookers. But even that room everything was veiled and hidden, as if the mystery in which they worked isolated them from the world.

Major Gentzel wiped a speck off his neat uniform and then asked:

"Did you want to see me?

Aleska took a moment to reply.

"Yes" he said at last. I have important reports to disclose to you.

Gentzel took out a page and a pen, preparing to write them down.

"Say, miss. I'll do the annotations myself. I don't want anyone to see her here. You are doing very useful work.

Aleska turned to look at the simple furniture in that office and told herself that this was reality. It was only that simple and austere room that counted.

"I know that the clandestine forces are preparing something important.

Gentzel nodded, adding:

"We go in parts. First of all, how do you know?

She, with an impassive face, explained:

"I was in the company of Stanislas Stychel all day. We talked and he gave me to understand that events were coming.

Gentzel made a few notes and asked again:

"What kind? They can be attacks or a resurgence of acts of sabotage.

She shook her head.

"I am inclined to believe that it is about something of greater importance.

Gentzel nodded.

"An uprising, then? Interesting.

"Remember" interrupted Aleska "that is just an impression of me.

"Your feedback has always been very helpful. And the idea of an uprising is not unreasonable.

"There is something else" she continued, referring to Stanislas' interest in staying at that inn and the unexpected appearance of Noraczewski to take him to Warsaw.

Gentzel lit a cigarette, having offered Aleska another, and was silent for a moment.

"This data is interesting," he said at last. Through another channel, we had confidences that the arrival of an important chief was expected. Although we do not know exactly which boss is the one that arrives. We do not know if it is General Komorowski or Colonel SS "He paused again and then asked:

"You have no idea?

Aleska shook her head.

"No, nor have I been able to identify this colonel.

Gentzel fiddled with the pen for a moment, then exclaimed:

"Of course, it is only a calculation, or rather an assumption, but could not the SS Colonel be your friend Stanislas Stychel? It has the same initials.

Aleska, unperturbed, shrugged.

"I ignore it.

"Well, we'll let you go anyway, and you try to find out what you can. His work is still as magnificent as ever.

* * *

Aleska, in her apartment, finished the cup of black tea that she had ordered for dinner and stretched out on the bed. He just wanted to close his eyes and wait for events to unfold. His will for nothing, he counted, driven by two different forces, such as duty and love.

She had come to Warsaw as an agent of her country's secret service, posing as a Swiss. He had studied in that country, and then, through the secret service, he got a job in Lucerne. There he had started his career as an agent. She was actually a spy. Never before had the infamous word been repeated, but at that moment he realized what it truly was.

When the conflict broke out, she wanted to serve Germany in some way and it seemed to her that entering as a nurse or as a telephone operator for the armed forces was not enough. There were many women who could do it. But she belonged to a family of soldiers and wanted to serve as one of them. He was not afraid and he was smart. Offered to the Abwehr.

Her relatives had advised her not to do so, but she was adamant. Once admitted, these same relatives, all of them soldiers, reminded her that duty was something that was above all personal consideration. From Switzerland, having discovered a spy ring, he went to France and then to the Balkans. Finally they sent her to Warsaw with the task of discovering everything related to the Clandestine Army.

They had given him Swiss documentation and a job with a Swiss company, to cover appearances. The rest was in his hands. Major Gentzel had known her for a long time and had great regard for her.

It also left him complete freedom in his movements, reminding him that he had always known how to succeed. With the reports that the Abwehr had provided, Aleska became involved with the Nationalists.

The fight was established in the same conditions. If she was an agent who concealed her personality, they also hid theirs, and while pretending to be simple employees or workers, they hid the offensive weapon in their house, waiting for the moment to attack the enemy. Acts of sabotage and attacks were happening continuously. Aleska had no qualms about fighting those civilians who had declared war on the soldiers of their homeland.

One day he met Stanislas Stychel. He guessed that he was some important personage in the enemy ranks and became intimate with him. Stanislas did not hide his opinions.

But as they became intimate, Aleska realized, although she did not want to admit it, that she was falling in love with that man. He fought desperately against this feeling.

He understood, he loved her too. And that afternoon they had confessed their love for each other.

He should have told him that he did not love him, but he lacked the strength to do so. And yet he had once again betrayed him to his superiors.

Perhaps Major Gentzel would decide to capture him, and then, with his declaration, he would be committed to a prison camp or perhaps shot as a sniper.

He covered his forehead with his hands. What could I do? Would it have been preferable for her to separate from Stanislas, letting him forget her, to ask for another destiny? This would have been tantamount to defecting. Or should she have kept quiet about what he revealed to her?

That would have amounted to treason. Desperate, she buried her face in the pillow, bursting into tears.

CHAPTER VI

PREPARATIONS

Stanislas was walking down the narrow corridor, led by a tall, muscular man in his leather raincoat. He had to show his documentation and give the password to be let through.

At last they came to a large cellar, at the door of which two men in civilian clothes stood guard with automatic weapons.

Stychel's escort saluted the head of the guard and announced:

"Colonel SS

The head of the guard checked the identity of the newcomer and then smiled apologetically:

"You have to take a lot of precautions.

"I understand," Stanislas said.

Shortly after, he entered a large, poorly lit cellar. Several men had gathered there.

They were all dressed in civilian clothes, wearing some coats with fur collars, frayed by use, or leather raincoats. All of them showed the signs on their faces of an active and intense life, full of dangers. Young or middle-aged, they all had in common the hard gesture and the straight, blazing gaze.

Their clothes also sometimes did not match the distinguished features of their faces. Many of them, who wore shabby suits, had elegant features.

In the center was a lean man, with tan skin and light hair, a cool, cool expression, and a determined air. It was General Bor-Komorowski, and the men who made up his staff, chiefs of the unit for the most part.

Stanislas sat down on a drawer, just as he had been instructed. The general stood up and cleared his throat. Then he was saying:

"Circumstances can help us or hurt us, depending on how we behave.

His dry, clear voice instilled a wave of enthusiasm in his followers. That man was a professional military man. Lieutenant colonel when the invasion of Poland broke out, he had been an obscure regimental leader forgotten among the hundreds of units that fought on the double front against the Germans and the Russians.

At the end of the campaign he managed to escape to the prison camps and began to prepare the clandestine fight. Little by little his exploits were giving his figure an aura of heroism, and the exiled Government in London had news of the existence of Colonel Bor-Komorowski, He was given command of the forces in Warsaw, His performance during those years had been a continuous succession of escapes and heroism, until the two groups that operated in that area were reunited.

Neither his figure nor his appearance implied his courage and his determination.

"We have" said "specific orders to anticipate the Russians and conquer Warsaw to present a Polish army alongside the Allied troops. General Anders' forces would be transported to Poland. But we must act before the Russians cross the Polish border. Therefore, I have decided that we rise up against the occupation troops.

There was a movement of enthusiasm among those who listened to him. Neither thought of the dangers he was going to face. If the general ordered it, they would assault the Komandatur on the way out.

"We have abundant material" Bor-Komorowski continued "and with enough volunteers. Presumably, once they are up, a large part of the population will join us, so it is important to have weapons for them. We must not think about the German arms depots, since General Schellenberg will have his arrangements in place in case we take over the city. On the day of the uprising "continued after a pause", the partisan groups operating in the vicinity of the city will gather in Warsaw. The rest must intensify their fight against the enemy troops, to prevent reinforcements from coming to the aid of the garrison.

"Likewise, during the remaining days, some groups will carry out various actions, aimed at hindering the repression of the uprising. I will give you specific orders, but I can tell you that among these acts is the attack on the chief of the German army. "He paused again and added," He disgusts me as much as you do, but he must be annihilated. It's about Lieutenant Colonel von Ritcher. Your troops have been very effective in the pursuit of our men and it must be prevented. I think Colonel S, S. should be in charge of commanding these groups.

Stanislas nodded.

"I will do whatever you order, sir general.

Bor-Komorowski continued:

"The date of the uprising will be August 1. Our objective is to paralyze the German garrison, which is why, first of all, it is necessary to cut all communication through the Vistula and then occupy the railway stations. The uprising will begin in the center of the Stare Miasto, that is, exactly in the Market Square, in Piekielko Square and in the Cathedral. From there they will depart to the two places indicated above. To cut the Vistula by Svelna Street and by the Alexander Bridge those who go to the Prague district. The first will be under the command of Major H. and the second, who will have to be in charge of the defense of an entire neighborhood, of Colonel SS

Those indicated agreed, taking data in a page. Then the general continued:

"The forces of Colonel« Tomorrow »will march towards Nowe Miasto, on Miodewa Street. The biggest "Night" will take care of the Krakow neighborhood, by Sajorna Square. The biggest Bolis will advance towards the Nowy Swiat and down the avenue Ujazdow. Bear in mind that in these more modern neighborhoods it will be very difficult to defeat the Germans, who, as the streets are wider, will be able to deploy their troops better. For this reason, we will make the old neighborhoods strong point, establishing our bases there. Colonel "Wladimir" will be in charge of these modern neighborhoods.

He paused and then asked:

"Is there any question?

Stanislas got to his feet.

"I would like to know if we have to fight until the Germans leave Warsaw or if there is an agreement to receive aid.

The general nodded.

"There is a very vague agreement about help. As I have told you, it is about landing General Anders' forces. On the other hand, it is preferable that we count on expelling the Germans and being able to gather all the partisan groups in Warsaw. Bear in mind that Warsaw is a communications hub and that by cutting them off, the Germans will not be able to send troops to fight against the Russians. If they are between two fires, they will have to surrender, which is not easy, or try to save as many forces as possible, evacuating the sector. Nothing more. Keep in mind what you have to do and divide your forces so that the blow does not miss. Bear in mind that this is the fate of Poland.

CHAPTER VII

BEFORE DEATH

Peter was humming a song, sitting inside a tent. The night stretched over Warsaw. Due to the proximity of the front, the public lighting was off, as the Russian planes bombed frequently. Through the dark streets, the car sped toward the lieutenant colonel's quarters.

Jüp, the Herculean orderly, led the vehicle, whistling happily. Next to Peter, Captain Schulz, his assistant, was silent. The young officer was concerned. He didn't like this service, but like his boss, he obeyed orders. On the other hand, he was aware that important events were coming and felt that he was not in the front line.

He would have liked to be like his boss, who never let his thoughts glimpse and who never disturbed his serenity.

Like every night, they returned to the barracks after having stayed with other officers in a nightclub on the outskirts.

From time to time the glow of the cigarette he was smoking lit up Lieutenant Colonel von Ritcher's face.

The noise of the engine rose in the silence of the night, advancing towards the interior of the neighborhood where the barracks rose.

Stanislas, hidden behind a corner, licked his lips. In the back of the pocket of his leather raincoat he kept the pistol.

Stychel glanced at the men, ten in all, who were standing a short distance behind the houses. Another group, somewhat larger, was arranged in such a way as to warn of the arrival of any German patrol.

It was the moment chosen to prepare for the attack on Lieutenant Colonel von Ritcher. Stanislas felt a certain disgust for this work, but he remembered the general's words. This officer had to stop capturing groups of partisans.

Captain Noraczewski stood beside him, motionless and silent. The Poles knew that the colonel passed by every night and that, as if he wanted to defy a possible danger, he never altered or varied his path.

A partisan approached, saying:

"Sir Colonel; it's coming.

Stanislas leaned toward his subordinate.

"Are you sure this is Colonel von Ritcher?

"It is a German field car. We cannot be wrong.

"Agree.

Stanislas approached the road and saw the vehicle speeding forward. His men were stationed, cocking their weapons. A cart pulled by an old horse crossed the street at that moment and a wheel seemed to break. He was stopped, preventing the passage, while the carter pretended to battle with the carriage.

Jüp turned to Peter, saying:

"There is a stopped car.

"Well" answered the young man. Stand up and ask if we can help you.

The orderly stopped the vehicle and stuck his head out the window. In bad Polish, he asked:

"We can help you? What happens?

The man pretended not to hear him and turned around, standing behind the car.

Stanislas waved and a partisan pulled the trigger of a submachine gun. He rattled the gun, spraying the car with lead.

Jüp grunted and exclaimed:

"They are attacking us, my lieutenant colonel.

He opened the car door and slipped out, clutching the submachine gun beside him.

Schulz drew the automatic, preparing to face the assailants. Peter just said:

"Let's hide behind the car.

The other partisans took up their weapons, starting to fire on the car. Stanislas encouraged them aloud:

"Let's go guys. Finish as soon as possible.

Ritcher got out of the car without removing the cigarette from his lips. The wisps of smoke were rising towards the sky and the glow of the cigar illuminated his face. Pistol in hand, he took cover behind the car and began to fire. Schulz, next to him, kept firing at the assailants, whom he did not see.

The partisans advanced, scattering to offer less target. They hid behind corners and terrain features. The lieutenant colonel had to be killed as soon as possible, as the shots would attract the attention of the German patrol.

Stanislas made out Ritcher's slim and elegant figure, tucked into his cloak and covered by his military cap. The cigarette hung from his lips, revealing him in the glow, but he was still firing, as if he were at target practice.

Suddenly a partisan collapsed, crying out in pain, Jüp aimed the submachine gun around a corner and pulled the trigger. The clatter disappeared, drowned out by the boom of weapons. But there were several screams of pain.

"Bravo, Jüp" exclaimed Peter. Every day you have better aim.

A silhouette moved in the distance and Peter fired the pistol twice.

Beside Stychel, Noraczewski slumped, hit on one shoulder. Stanislas bent to pick him up. The wounded had to be removed from there before the German patrols arrived.

A partisan took a grenade and threw it with full force on the car. There was an explosion and the three Germans slammed into the vehicle.

Peter raised his head to see what had happened. Jüp writhed in pain on the floor. Peter, without letting go of the gun, leaned toward him, saying:

"Schulz, take the machine gun.

The captain obeyed, firing at the partisans. Ritcher sat the soldier upright.

"How are you boy?

The soldier's eyes narrowed.

"They have screwed me, my lieutenant colonel. But I have taken some ahead.

"Do not move. We will heal you.

Peter sat up, tossing the nearly consumed cigarette to the ground. Several partisans, hit by the captain's shots, lay on the ground. Ritcher fired back.

A partisan approached Stanislas.

"The sentries warn that some German patrols are approaching.

"It's okay. We will withdraw!

Word spread and the partisans moved away, carrying the wounded, while the whistles of enemy patrols sounded in the distance.

Peter raised his head. The attack had already passed. He took out a cigarette and lit it, placing it between the wounded man's lips.

"A little calm Jüp. They are here and we will heal you.

CHAPTER VIII

MAYBE FOR THE LAST TIME

Noraczewski sat up in bed, asking:

"When can I get out of here?

The doctor, also a member of the Clandestine Army, smiled.

"Soon, don't get upset.

Stanislas accompanied the doctor to the door. He smiled.

"By the first of August it will be completely fine.

Stanislas nodded, closing the door. Then he returned to the wounded man. The captain begged:

"Tell me the truth, Colonel.

"Yes man. That you can join us. There are still three days to go.

* * *

Peter put his hand to his visor as he passed the coffin containing Jüp's remains. He had died. His orderly, the faithful companion of his fighting hours, was gone forever. He was his liaison when the war broke out and he commanded only one company. She never wanted to be separated from him and then death, the soldier's eternal companion, took the faithful Jüp. What battles of the magnitude of Moscow and Dunkirk did not achieve, an ambush of partisans did.

The drums beat, while the coffin was to be buried. The sad, martial notes of "I had a comrade" they rose above the cemetery. Peter, firm, with his hand on the visor, was saying goodbye to his brother in arms.

* * *

Stanislas looked at his watch. Aleska was late. He was in the same restaurant where they used to meet, and although he had been ordered not to go out alone, he had come to meet her. The captain did not get out of bed and did not want anyone else to know her.

The young man realized that it might be dangerous for the girl to cross those narrow streets, excited as they were. They could take her for German and in the previous days there had been several altercations. But he couldn't go longer without seeing her.

The door opened and Aleska walked into the restaurant smiling. The young man shook his hand.

"Let's get out of here" he proposed. The atmosphere is very charged.

She nodded and together they went out into the street. The buildings of the old city were close together, preventing the passage of vehicles. Stanislas told himself that it would be easy to fight the German troops there.

Suddenly he felt the girl's hand rest on his arm. He turned to her, smiling at her.

"What's wrong? Aleska asked. You seem worried.

Stanislas smiled.

"Nothing happens to me.

They continued on their way in silence, until they reached another restaurant, almost empty. A waiter in a worn tailcoat seated them at one end of the room.

They looked at each other in silence, smiling. Aleska raised her hand to caress her cheek.

"Why don't you tell me what you have?

The young man accentuated his smile, shaking his head.

"It's just that nothing happens to me. Everything is your figuration.

The waiter served them the drinks, oblivious to everything that was not his job.

Aleska stroked his forehead, while saying:

"You seem concerned. You have a fixed gaze, as if something obsessed you.

The young man shook his head.

"Well, yes: I am concerned about the war. Nobody knows how it will end.

She smiled.

"In this I cannot relieve you. I know nothing about wars or military things.

Stanislas nodded.

"Of which I am very happy. Since I was a child, I have done nothing but deal with military matters. "He paused and added," The only thing that really matters is that I love you very much.

Aleska smiled, approaching him.

"Me too darling. I had never thought of coming to Warsaw and could not imagine that I was going to give my heart here.

The young man shook his hand and then added:

"But I'm worried that ...

She covered his mouth with her hands.

"You shouldn't worry about anything. We love each other and we are happy. The rest should not even be mentioned.

The hours passed slowly between them. Stanislas couldn't get the idea from his mind that it was the last time they'd seen each other. Within three days they would rise up in arms against the German garrison and fight until they took over the city. He couldn't think of her until the moment he had won. During the battles that would follow the uprising, many things could happen and he might die. But it was the luck of the soldiers.

He was not going to tell Aleska anything about the uprising, nor about the danger that could happen. He would already find out what was happening.

In the next three days he would be too busy to see her and should focus all his attention on the events that were to come.

But the idea that perhaps, even if she ignored it, this interview was a farewell, pressed her heart like a stone. He clasped the girl's hands tightly, trying to control her uneasiness. He only had to think about the work that awaited him. He knew its importance and did not want to fail.

At last they realized the lateness of the hour and Aleska warned:

"It would be convenient for me to go home. It's late and the German patrols are asking for the documentation.

Stychel nodded. He stood up, placing a few coins on the table. Then he took the girl by the arm and went out into the street.

They went on for a moment in silence. At last the young man exclaimed:

"Aleska, I must leave Warsaw. I'll call you as soon as I get back.

The girl nodded. The Pole said again:

"The war is very close to Warsaw. If something happens, whatever it is, take refuge in the Embassy of your country.

Aleska looked at him in amazement.

"What can happen?

He excused himself:

"If the Germans fell back and the city was unguarded, the undesirables would plunder. During the bombings it is also possible that they do so. Do you promise me that you'll be careful?

"Of course.

They had reached the vicinity of the pension where she lived. The young man kissed her on the cheek and then watched her walk away, until she was lost in the shadows of the night. He had to succeed as soon as possible to be able to rejoin her. Perhaps, he told himself, he would never see her again. He made an effort, wrenching everything but the coming uprising from his mind.

CHAPTER IX

THE NIGHT OF AUGUST 1

That night, in many homes in Warsaw, no one slept. Others went on with their lives as usual, not understanding what was coming.

But in many houses women and children gathered around the images, praying for the men who left their homes and marched to congregate at the Stare Miasto.

Many rebels did not go to their homes, meeting in nearby bars and taverns.

Little by little the hours of the night were closing in on Warsaw, spreading the shadows over the narrow medieval streets. Some hid in the residence of companions waiting for the moment to go to the appointment with death and adventure.

In the weapons centers, the sentries licked their lips, hoping to distribute the rifles and machine guns to those engaged.

The chiefs studied the plans and read the orders once more, preparing to carry them out.

A nervous and threatening silence spread throughout the Stare Miasto. A silence that heralded death and destruction.

The German patrols continued their journey, rifles on their shoulders, looking from side to side, following the severe orders they had received.

In their flat, Stanislas, Dmowaki, and Noraczewski were smoking silently, waiting, waiting.

Stychel remembered Aleska once more, trusting that they would soon see each other again.

At last, Dmowaki exclaimed:

"It is time now.

They came off the floor, pulling on their raincoats. The night imposed a warm garment. The three pocketed their pistols, preparing to face danger.

Throughout the Stare Miasto the men involved in the uprising were marching towards the meeting points. Through the narrow streets they advanced in groups of three or four, trying to avoid the German patrols, and headed towards their points of concentration.

At the appointed time, the different units had gathered at the intersections that led to the Market Square, the Cathedral Square and Piekielko Square.

Then the chiefs of the forces appeared. They went on foot, since the cars could not move there, and they headed towards their points of concentration. Meanwhile, in an old warehouse, General Bor-Komorowski, surrounded by his staff, waited for the moment to start the battle.

At the appointed time for the uprising, a raucous "Long live Poland!" Was heard in the alleys of the center of the Old City, and the rebels, already equipped with their weapons, crossing their holsters, coats and raincoats, advanced to occupy strategic positions.

The chiefs, equipped like them, brandished their pistols, heading towards the places that needed to be conquered. In the buildings neighboring the three squares, the tenants watched in surprise what was happening.

Many rushed to join the rebels.

In the alleys near the mentioned squares, the vanguards of the rebels collided with some enemy patrols.

Gunfire crossed and hand bombs exploded. Combatants from both sides fell, but the patrols were forced to flee or disband. Little by little, the rebels were deployed throughout the Old City. Police posts and troop detachments were encircled by armed men who were shooting furiously at them. The heads of the posts telephoned their superiors, informing them of what was happening.

The partisan leaders, in the previously chosen houses, were planting machine guns and mortars, so that they dominated the alleys that reached there and prevented the advance of the Germans.

Others erected barricades at street crossings, building them with cobblestones and furniture taken from anywhere. Machine guns, mortars and light guns were also mounted there, awaiting the enemy advance.

The chiefs were occupying the telephone exchanges and choosing places to establish hospitals and quartermaster warehouses.

Volunteers came from all over the Old City to join the ranks of the Clandestine Army. In the parts of the city where the rebel forces had not yet arrived, the volunteers who had not attended the meeting waited for the moment to join their companions.

They were the detachments destined to fight against the Germans, attacking them from behind, once the rebellious forces had reached there.

The armed tide was spreading uncontrollably through the city, shaking it with its shots.

The German command, notified by telephone of what was happening, met at the Komandatur. General Schellenberg rallied his subordinates, preparing to face the uprising.

All were present, equipped with their war helmets and weapons. Only von Ritcher, with his helmet on his knees and his cigarette between his lips, seemed ready to attend a reception.

Schellenberg asked first of all:

"Have the orders I gave been carried out?

The chiefs rose one by one and reported that the units, under the command of the second chief, had been withdrawing towards the outskirts. The encircled groups were fighting desperately, trying to resist or break through. Warsaw was surrounded by a cordon of German troops.

Schellenberg explained:

"We are interested, above all, in maintaining communications over the Vistula and keeping the railway station in our hands so that we can continue to monitor the situation and have fast means of transportation. The telephone exchange, as far as possible, also interests us, so as not to lose contact. In any case, the communications troops will lay down makeshift phone lines. The powder kegs are in our hands, as well as the hospitals. That each boss remains in his position, preventing the enemy advance. It is necessary to dominate the Vistula line and drive the rebels away from the other shore.

Ritcher got to his feet.

"Aren't we going to try to save the encircled troops? They are soldiers who are fighting and can expect help from their comrades in arms.

Schellenberg passed his hand over his eyes.

"I don't think it is possible. You, Ritcher, will reinforce the Prague sector, to prevent the conquest of the station. Return each one to your command posts and maintain communication with me.

The chiefs saluted, preparing to depart. The general gestured to the young man.

"Peter" exclaimed ", do not think it does not hurt me to leave those boys. But we will warn the rebels to respect the lives of the prisoners.

"If they don't comply, they'll remember von Ritcher" said Peter, his serene face altered for the first time.

CHAPTER X

AVALANCHE

Major H's forces gathered next to a small square near Scelna Street. The river breeze came up to them and they saw the buildings overlooking the Vistula.

Major H, a short and sturdy man, reviewed his volunteers and deployed a large group of the vanguard, armed with his submachine guns.

They advanced down Scelna Street, clinging to the walls. It was easy to meet a German patrol or a detachment of troops.

The way was clear. They soon made out he laughed, with the boats moored to the docks. About five German policemen stood guard there, brandishing their rifles. The leader of the vanguard made a sign and the weapons began to bark. Two policemen collapsed without life, while the other three ran to defend themselves. Shots thundered, while the rebels spread out along the dock, making sure there were no more adversaries. The three policemen, sheltered behind bundles, fought hopelessly but tenaciously.

Other groups of Major H had entered the buildings overlooking the Vistula and planted machine guns and heavy mortars there, dominating the entire river. They could reach the opposite shore.

When Major H with his forces reached the dock, the three policemen had already been annihilated.

The major pointed out the most powerful barges and had machine guns planted in the bow.

Meanwhile, others were deployed along the dock, preparing to repel any enemy attack. Across the river stood the buildings of Nowe Miasto, reflecting in the water.

This waterway was the quickest and shortest way to transport troops and food from one end of the town to the other.

Major H was hesitant for a moment. He had studied his plan of attack over and over again, until he knew the smallest details by heart, and yet he was undecided now. In the various attempts to conquer the other shore of the no, he could lose many people. He contemplated those boys, full of enthusiasm and fervor, who might soon die. And maybe they all fell for his mistake.

At last he made them board the boats and ordered them to advance. In turn, the older one jumped onto one of them. Those who remained on the shore dismissed them, waving their hands, while from the floors they waved their caps in the air.

The launches were in motion, heading toward the neighboring shore. The men inside licked their lips as they caressed their weapons.

The nearest barges stopped their engines and waited for the momentum to carry them to shore. Suddenly a thunderous rifle fire broke out on the docks. Machine guns rattled, sending deadly charges toward the launches. The men stretched out inside the boats, waiting for the moment to jump ashore. Some were hit. It was seen how a barge, its sides slashed open by enemy fire, capsized as its occupants jumped into the water.

At last the first boats touched shore. Its occupants jumped to the ground. The silhouettes of the Germans charging were seen. Guns barked and hand grenades exploded.

The insurgents attacked with fury, laying down on the dock to be able to shoot better. Little by little they were asserting themselves on the dock. Machine guns planted on the barges opened fire.

The disembarked men began to spread out along the quay, fighting with the Germans. Hand grenades exploded and rifles and automatic weapons rattled, while combatants clashed frequently. Suddenly, a large group of armed civilians rushed to the scene of the fight, attacking the Germans from behind. It was the forces of that sector, joining the fight, according to the orders received.

Major H distributed his men and set up barricades, preparing to defend the conquered place. German launches must not be allowed to continue on the river.

Meanwhile, new volunteers, not included in the Clandestine Army, were going to the posts and the barricades. They were given the weapons of captured or killed Germans or were sent to command posts, where they could be armed and framed.

Colonel Tomorrow's forces, a smiling Herculean man, were marching down Miodewa Street, heading towards Nowe Miasto. The German forces had to retreat to avoid being encircled by the attacks of the two columns of volunteers who threatened to close them in a bag. Colonel "Tomorrow" was advancing through the old residential neighborhood, which once stood outside the walls, and taking corner by corner and street by street. They soon managed to establish contact with the troops of Major H.

The Krakow district offered some difficulty.

The older "Night," a thin, dark-looking man, but who knew how to get a lot out of the troops he commanded. The streets that ran from the Castle Square to the Saxony Square had been a concentration point for the police forces and troops who were strolling through the city. There they fought desperately, retreating in fairly order to Saxony Square. After the monument to José Pomatowski, some groups were placed, ready to die killing.

The biggest "Night" was destroying them group by group, reducing their resistance and cleaning the streets. At last, the Polish flag was raised over the José Pomatowski monument.

Nowy Swiat and Ujazdow Avenue were difficult to conquer. Major Bolis, young, well planted and determined, was maneuvering his troops through the wide arteries and gardens that surrounded them. From there, the fight was less easy. It was necessary to change tactics and throw the men towards the houses so that once they were conquered they would shoot down the street and force the Germans to retreat.

The most difficult thing was the conquest of the Modern Neighborhoods. The wide, uncluttered streets did not offer much protection for Colonel Wladimir's troops. He had to distribute his troops in small groups and send them to the assault, attacking the forces that offered them resistance. The streets parallel to the Vistula became a battlefield. The rebels took the cars and trucks they found, turning them into strongholds, so that they could advance well protected.

But the Germans were not prepared to give in where they were fighting with some advantage and they stuck to the corners and intersections, establishing a crossfire of machine guns and antitanks.

Time and again the Poles were thrown on the last line of resistance, established by the German colonel, trying to force it, but without success. The Modern Quarter became, overnight, the most cruel battlefield in all of Warsaw.

CHAPTER XI

Prague

Bor-Komorowski paced nervously but in control of his makeshift headquarters. Calls from the bosses reached him, informing him of their progress and their successes. Little by little, the assistants were pointing out on the great map of the city the points reached by the rebels.

The general did not alter his cold, energetic face. He realized that for the moment the desired objectives were being achieved and that it was not difficult for him to win in the city, dominating it completely. But it was an adventure that, as in all, the end was unknown.

Many imponderables, which were not in their power to solve, could decide victory or failure.

Bor-Komorowski approached his assistants and began typing on the table. They looked at him, waiting for a question or comment. The general only said:

"Navigation on the Vistula has been partially cut off. But we know nothing about the Prague district. What is Colonel SS doing? What will it be doing?

* * *

Stanislas threw the cigarette on the ground and ordered Major Dmowaki:

"The scouting party can advance.

Noraczewski, arm in a sling, approached, pleading:

"Let me send it to me, Colonel.

Stychel shook his head.

"I need you by my side and I cannot tolerate it.

Stanislas's forces had reached the vicinity of the Alexander Bridge. From the balconies and the tallest buildings, groups of Poles fired machine gun and rifle fire on the bridge, blocking the way for German troops. Likewise, from previously chosen places they threw mortars, which would impede their advance.

Stanislas had studied this sector thoroughly and had calculated the possibilities of advance. He knew that the Germans would hinder the march and that a single advance attempt would be instantly stopped.

Dmowaki placed a strong party next to the bridge, at the other end of which were the Germans, firing incessantly. Other groups were heading towards the river, embarking on barges. It was time to start the advance. Stychel beckoned. Automatic weapons and mortars increased their fire, lengthening the shot to reach only the other shore.

Meanwhile, the boats and barges began to cross the river, all protected by the shadows of the night.

Stanislas stood motionless by the balustrade of the bridge, waiting for news of those first groups to arrive. He knew what this could matter and it was necessary for him to achieve it. If he did not conquer the station, fresh troops would soon arrive in Warsaw and the uprising would end in terrible failure.

The night made it impossible to see how the barges were moving away towards the other shore and how the patrols were advancing, deployed on the bridge, but the colonel knew that his men were not going to fail him. Suddenly shots were heard at the other end of the bridge, as well as a shout from the opposite bank.

All the rebels leaned forward, caressing their weapons. Perhaps the time had come. The shooting increased in intensity, but no one could tell what was happening. However, while the rebels remained nervous waiting for what was going to happen, they realized that the rumor of the battle was slowly fading away.

A partisan came running to meet Stanislas.

"Sir Colonel" he said, "we have managed to establish ourselves on the other shore.

Stychel rested his hand on the liaison's shoulder and turned to his men, who stood confusedly around the corners and along the bridge. He waved his arm and ran across the bridge. A thunderous cheer rose behind him, as the rebels ran at full speed after their leader or threw themselves on the barges to cross the river.

Stanislas, pistol in hand, was advancing towards the other end of the bridge, where shots continued to be heard. His volunteers followed him, waving their rifles in the air.

At last they reached the opposite shore. Stychel turned to the river to look at the stream. The groups of barges were gathering almost alongside the shore.

He continued on, soon catching up with his partisans. The Germans had been thrown from their posts and could already spread out along the shore.

The reinforcements helped the rebels a lot. Soon they began to spread through the streets and around corners, attacking the Germans. The barges had deposited their loads of men, who were running to join the Poles already stationed there.

The heavy weapons were partly transported to the other shore, to continue fighting. Little by little the groups, well led by Stychel, spread out through the city, heading for the station.

Dawn was beginning to dye the sky red, when the rebels made out the gray and dirty buildings of the station. A cry of enthusiasm rose from her breasts.

Among them ran the slogan:

"One more effort and we have won."

Through the streets, jumping from window to window and from patio to patio, rebels and soldiers were attacking each other relentlessly, in a continuous battle.

They spread out down a wide, lonely avenue, heading for the station. Stanislas closely followed the first vanguards. It was necessary to occupy the railway station, the axis of all the lines, to be able to dominate the network of railways that led there.

Shots rang out and machine guns rattled, spreading their death barks. Stychel watched as detachments approached the vast gray building, covered by the patina of age and the smoke of hundreds of steam engines.

The German grenadiers were fighting desperately, but were cornered by partisans who jumped on them from windows and through walls. Numerous volunteers left their homes, taking weapons from the dead or from prisoners.

Soon, Stychel told himself, they would have occupied the station. Dawn spread its milky white light everywhere, giving the outlines a ghostly appearance.

They had already opened a breach in the enemy defense and the first vanguards had already entered the station. It was being fought within her and they would soon be able to dominate her.

Suddenly there was a sound of engines and a column of cars equipped with antiaircraft machine guns and with light medium tanks and auto-machine guns was seen advancing in the direction of the railway station.

Someone announced:

"They are von Ritcher's troops.

Almost before the vehicles stopped, the "hunters" jumped to the ground, raising their weapons, at the same time that the tanks began to fire and went on the insurgents.

Stanislas gave his orders quickly. It was necessary to hold on and avoid being surrounded by those audacious and fierce troops, accustomed to blows and surprises.

The station became the hub of combat. Both of them battled to preserve it or to conquer it, while the rest of the forces took up positions that seemed most appropriate to them.

Stychel made out the graceful silhouette of an officer, cigarette between his lips, directing, serene and calm under the bullets, the movement of his men.

The thrust of the tanks and the hunters forced the rebels to abandon the station, but Stanislas had placed the machine and mortar servants in such a way that the Germans could not occupy it.

The fighting continued fierce, but the station remained in no man's land, without the Germans being able to use it and without the Poles being able to render it useless. Neither of them could call her theirs and neither of them had failed. The fight began, unnerving and cruel. Relentlessly attacking each other with ferocity.

Food was distributed under enemy fire and the wounded had to be cared for under enemy bullets.

But after the first surprise, the two sides prepared to resist, until one gave up.

CHAPTER XII

AN IMPORTANT MISSION

Aleska entered Major Gentzel's office. The veteran smiled, indicating a chair.

The girl obeyed, lighting a cigarette. The uprising had lasted for several days and nothing was known about the operations. The battles and fights in the streets continued daily, without anyone being able to know what fate the future held for them.

Major Gentzel passed a hand across his forehead and smiled again. Except for this gesture of fatigue, no one could have imagined that this cold and impersonal man felt concerned about events.

"The uprising" he began to say "was an initial success for General Bor-Komorowski. That cannot be denied. It achieved almost all of its objectives, but it failed to spread further. However, at present both sides have fortified ourselves and we continue to shoot and fight, to see which of the two dominates the other. At this time, when the Russian offensive acquires its greatest strength, this uprising can be final for our weapons. It must be completed as soon as possible.

Aleska nodded, hoping the older man would give the reason for calling her.

"A very important point is the station in the Prague district. If the Poles could use it, they could bring groups of partisans here from the countryside. This would increase your chances of success. At the moment, neither one nor the other dominate it, being only a goal for both of them.

Aleska nodded again. No one could imagine the tension in which she had lived during those days, always thinking about Stanislas and what might happen to him. He knew that this uprising was the end of his love affairs. Whoever triumphs, they should separate definitively.

"The Prague sector" continued Gentzel "is defended by the forces of Colonel S, S.

The girl, interested, raised her head.

"Have they managed to identify him? "I ask.

"Yes, we have finally made it. It's about an old friend of hers.

Aleska blinked in amazement.

"Who is it?

"Stanislas Stychel.

The young woman's heart skipped a beat.

"Are you sure? I could never imagine that they were the same person.

Gentzel nodded.

"Neither you nor anyone else could imagine it. You have to recognize the skill and bravery of that man. He knew how to deceive us to the end and it was he who made fun of us. Now it is his prestige and his military capacity that sustains the Prague district. Without him, we could have occupied the station and expelled them back to Stare Miasto. "He paused and added," There is a way to do it, and you can offer it to us.

Aleska was afraid, without knowing why. With his eyes he invited the older man to speak.

"You can get to Colonel Stychel and tell us where his command post is located. We know that it is very close to what we might call the first line. Once informed of this, we would send a group determined to capture him. In this way, all the resistance in Prague would collapse.

Aleska shuddered. It was she, precisely she, who had to give captive the man she loved, Stanislas. But Gentzel knew nothing of her feelings. She had volunteered for the Secret Service and had a duty to fulfill, as a front-line soldier.

The older's cold gray pupils stared at her. He must give an answer. The girl felt tortured by a thousand contradictory feelings. She remembered her father and her brothers, who were fighting at the head of their troops. He thought of all the lives he could save. However, he could not decide.

Something had to happen to avoid what they asked of him and that he could not refuse, Gentzel asked again:

"What's wrong with him?

Aleska heard a voice, which was not hers, say to her:

"I will do what I can, Major Gentzel.

* * *

Stanislas, in his command post, ate some preserves that had been brought to him from headquarters. His assistants and sentries had the same food as him. Sitting on the ground, they devoured the ranch, with the rifle at their side.

Stychel wondered what would become of Aleska and what she was doing right now. He will never forget her.

By a tank, Ritcher ate a sandwich handed to him by an orderly and downed a glass of hot tea. The helmet fit snugly around his soldier's head. The lieutenant colonel was concerned about the fate of the battle. But he had to admit that those Poles were good fighters.

In the rest of the city, the fighting continued with equal fierceness and ferocity. Around the river and in the wide streets of the Modern Neighborhoods, rapid weapons and bayonets, along with light cannons, worked tirelessly over and over again.

The uprising continued, without anyone seeing a way to end it quickly.

CHAPTER XIII

UNDER THE BLANKET OF WAR

Major Gentzel jumped out of the car and helped Aleska out. The girl, huddled in her coat, gazed out at the streets and buildings, stained by the dawn light, looming before her like military fortifications. He made out the silhouettes of the grenadiers of his country, with the rifle in their hands and their helmets firmly attached.

In front of them were Stanislas's men fighting desperately.

Gentzel repeated:

"It is better that you do not go directly to the Prague district. Through this sector you can easily reach the rebel lines, and once there ask to see Stanislas Stychel. They will lead her to him.

The older man held out his hand and added:

"Good luck lady.

The girl nodded and went away in the direction of the place where the rebels were.

Cautiously, he hid around corners and doorways. They could not expose themselves to the Poles knowing that the German troops allowed them to pass.

* * *

A partisan approached Stanislas, saying:

Colonel, a girl wishes to see you.

Stanislas raised his head.

"What do you want?

"He has not said.

"Well, let it happen.

The partisan left and shortly after Aleska entered the command post. The girl stared at Stanislas, not sure what role to take. Stychel got to his feet and ran to her.

"Aleska, what are you doing here? He exclaimed, holding out his hands.

"I couldn't stay apart from you any longer. I managed to get to your lines and asked to be brought to see you.

The assistants had come out and were alone. Stanislas hugged her, pulling her closer.

"I should not allow you to remain here, since you are in danger.

She closed her eyes and leaned her head on the chest of the man she loved and was about to betray. She regretted being there, and yet no one had forced her to join the Secret Service.

Stanislas stroked her hair, adding:

"I was afraid I would never see you again. I don't know how this fight will end, which lasts longer than it should. It's been fifteen days since everything started.

Aleska raised her hands to caress the face of the rebel.

"All I wanted was to be by your side. I don't care about the rest. Let's not talk about the future. It only matters that we are together and that we can finally wait, side by side, for this to end.

Stanislas kissed her, holding her tightly against his chest. She wrapped her arms around his neck, as if she intended to give her life in that kiss and thus erase the barrier that separated them.

He realized that he was committing the most despicable betrayal on a woman. Major Gentzel was unaware that Stychel loved her, but she knew it. However, he had accepted the mission assigned to him.

But she was a soldier and she knew that soldiers could not allow particular reasons to get in the way of duty. Stanislas himself had done so. But what would this sincere and determined man say when he found out that she was taking advantage of his feelings to sell him? I would never believe in her love. I would imagine that it was all a ruse to defeat and arrest him.

And never in her life had the girl felt such a strong and passionate love as the one that consumed her for Stychel.

Stanislas looked at her smiling.

"I am glad to have you by my side, but I prefer that you stay away from danger. This is no place for a woman.

Aleska shook her head.

"I will not allow you to push me away. I have seen women taking care of the wounded and distributing food and ammunition. There are even some volunteers.

"But they are Polish and you are a foreigner. This fight has nothing to do with you.

The girl was slow to respond. Stanislas could not imagine that this fight involved her too, but on the enemy side.

"I want to be by your side" he murmured.

Stanislas did not reply, merely hugging her against him, while outside machine guns rattled and mortars thundered.

* * *

Aleska had been in the rebel camp for several days. The situation had not improved for either the Poles or the Germans. Both conserved the positions that they conquered the first days and only some intersections and some buildings changed hands daily.

The girl was already a familiar figure to the partisans. Accustomed to seeing her take care of the wounded and tend to the food, they were not disturbed when they saw her pass. In these jobs, Aleska put all her effort perhaps to get tired and not be able to think about what she was going to do.

He had studied the situation and realized how easy it was to carry out the coup. Stanislas had established his command post in a small building, which belonged to the railway staff. It had two rooms and was full of tools that were handed over to the partisans.

He was almost in the line of fire; a line of combat that extended by intersections, stretches of track and machine-gunned buildings. It would not be difficult, from where the troops were, to launch a mass attack and capture the chief. Or send a chosen squad and conquer the house by assault.

She didn't know what they were going to do, but she wouldn't leave Stanislas. She felt the young man's gaze full of tenderness, that not once did he stop looking at her.

He had not yet found a way to deliver his message to the German forces, but he hoped to do so soon.

Stanislas used to stay there all night, except when he went out on his rounds.

But between nine and eleven he was always found.

Aleska preferred not to think about the future. She knew that her love was going to die assassinated by herself and this certainty made her despair, with a deep anguish. There was no way to avoid what was coming.

Stanislas felt happy and, at the same time, scared to have her there, next to the danger. But perhaps it would have been worse not to have her by his side and not know what had happened to her.

It seemed to him that he knew how to fight better and that he was more lucid in directing his men.

Meanwhile, the Battle of Warsaw continued, cruel and fierce, with no end in sight. From one end of the city to the other, men attacked each other fiercely, seeking the means of success. The population that had not intervened in the fight remained in their homes, waiting for everything to end. Life had come to a standstill.

In the areas occupied by the rebels, bread and food were distributed, taken from the captured warehouses. The same thing was done in the area occupied by the troops, but the ghost of hunger was beginning to spread over Warsaw.

CHAPTER XIV

CHANGE OF COMMAND

A field car pulled up in front of the Komandatur. The sentry at the door, with a critical eye, realized that an important person was traveling inside.

The orderly jumped to the ground and opened the door, squaring himself stiffly. This ended up convincing the sentry that the character traveling inside was not just anybody.

A general got out of the vehicle, heading with a determined step towards the house. He was still a young man, stout and strong. His uniform was clean and well cut, but it had traces of the dust from the journey. On his chest he wore various decorations, some from the war of 1914. Under the plaid cap, a flushed countenance and energetic features stood out, highlighting his willful chin and fiery pupils.

His assistants seemed as determined and tough men as he.

He responded to the sentry's salute and informed the officer of the watch that it was General Bach-Zelewski, who had just arrived from the Russian front.

Everyone shuddered when they heard the name of the military man. This determined and fearless soldier was always on the battle line and ready to move forward, no matter what the difficulties were.

He had specialized in hard shots and difficult situations. He was also famous for his booming voice when giving orders under enemy fire.

He was greeted by Schellenberg and his assistant. Bach-Zelewski squared himself, displaying an office from the Grand Headquarters, in which he was appointed chief of all the Warsaw forces, under Schellenberg.

"My general" he continued, with his somewhat brusque way of speaking, "I am not here to replace anyone, nor to spoil anyone's work. I await orders.

Schellenberg could not contain a smile at that manner of speaking so characteristic of the stormtrooper commander.

"The situation" he began to say, approaching the plan of the city that hung on the wall "is not promising, but it is not hopeless either. We are in a waiting period, in which we do not see a solution in the near future.

"I have been charged at the Headquarters to put down the uprising soon. This makes it difficult to send troops to the front lines, and this is not the time for delays. The Russians continue to advance towards the Polish border. It has been almost a month since the uprising broke out. Isn't that so, my general?

Schellenberg nodded.

"So so. However, the difficulty is that it is difficult to dislodge the rebels from their points of resistance, since the neighborhoods have to be conquered house by house. Are you bringing reinforcements?

"Only a battalion of tanks" answered Bach-Zelewski "and a mortar of 65. I think this will suffice.

Schellenberg then said:

"I suppose you are tired. This afternoon we can bring the staff together and discuss these matters.

The newcomer shook his head.

"I am not tired, my general. We can meet as soon as possible.

Two hours later, all the unit chiefs were assembled in the Komandatur. Major Gentzel and Colonel Haller were also there with the general. Also in the meeting was a smiling lieutenant colonel, his face tanned by the sun, wearing the skull of the armored troops.

"General Bach-Zelewski" began to say Schellenberg "will take command of the forces in the square. We must first of all prepare an examination of the situation.

The chief of staff read a report prepared with the parts of the different unit chiefs, explaining the situation of the contending forces. Bach-Zelewski listened silently, tapping a pencil on the table. He was using more and more force to do it.

The tanker chief, a former friend of Peter, said to him:

"He is getting furious. He will end up punching the table.

"They say he has a very bad temper" replied Peter.

"Of course. It's awful. But you can be sure that the uprising will be crushed.

When he finished, Bach-Zelewski rose to his feet.

"From what I just said, the two nerve centers of the city are the river and the Prague district. Therefore, it is necessary to push the rebels to the other side of the Vistula and to resume river communications. Then it is necessary to expel them from the station, so that the trains can circulate freely. "He turned to Schellenberg and added," If that's okay with you, sir, we will carry out these two operations first and then we will press on the Old City until they are forced to surrender or until they are annihilated.

Schellenberg smiled at her fieryness.

"This is what has been tried, without success so far. They stick to the ground and resist well.

"I see it, my general, but I think we can employ means other than those employed up to now. Tanks and flamethrowers will be very useful to us. This house-to-house and street-to-street fighting is much like the ones we endured in Stalingrad and in the conquest of the fortifications of Sevastopol. Infantry forces need to be flexible and fight well; something like our paratroopers and enemy commandos. But I have also been able to verify that the bravest man, capable of assaulting a machine gun nest with bare chest, feels frightened by a flamethrower. It will be necessary to provide them to the combatants. Tanks are almost invincible because they constitute a mobile bulwark which can only be defeated with cannons against tanks, of which it is not easy for the rebels to dispose of in quantity.

Peter smiled, looking at the head of the panzers. Major Gentzel stood up and cleared his throat, saying:

"It would be convenient to inform the rebels that they are going to be crushed and that it is better that they surrender. Enclosures could be formed to accommodate them, along with the entire civilian population that wishes to come to our lines.

"Sounds good to me," said Schellenberg, when asked by Bach-Zelewski. Colonel Haller will see to you.

"My general" continued Major Gentzel, "we have trustworthy confidences of the place where the command post of Colonel SS, chief of the rebels in the area of the station, is located. We have taken aerial photographs to get to know the house well. The pilot who took them was shot several times, but was unharmed. I believe, unless you think otherwise, that a well-chosen squad can capture you and deprive the enemy of one of their best leaders.

Bach-Zelewski turned to Schellenberg:

"If you do not object, my general, I believe that this measure could be carried out. "When the superior nodded, he asked": What unit could be in charge of this mission?

"Lieutenant Colonel von Ritcher.

CHAPTER XV

AGAIN FRONT TO FRONT

Dawn was coming. On the gray roofs of the city the dawn was announcing, while in the intersections and on the corners men fought and waited for the battle to continue.

Peter engaged his battalion's assault patrol. The second lieutenant in command greeted her, saying:

"No news, my lieutenant colonel.

Von Ritcher motioned for him to lower his hand, then explained:

"You all know what is expected of you. You have studied the photographs and the plan of the sector. You know which house we must raid and also the man who must be captured or killed. I'll send the patrol myself.

Among the men of that unit there was a movement of satisfaction. They stroked their submachine guns and rifles, puffing out their chests. Handguns and pistols wore on the belt. Ritcher picked up a submachine gun and muttered:

"Go.

Captain Schulz watched him walk away, licking his lips. He was not afraid that this operation would end in failure. The only thing he feared was that his boss would die in the fight.

The patrol advanced to the last sentry posts. The "hunters" smiled, muttering:

Good luck, comrades.

A sergeant raised his hand, smiling.

Peter looked at the narrow lane at the end of which the Poles stood. Between both positions a lot was opened. Hopefully, they could cross to the other side without anyone noticing.

Von Ritcher beckoned and the men jumped over the fence, entering the lot. They had abandoned their heavy weapons and only kept those that could be useful in close combat.

Major Wagner, second battalion commander, turned to Schulz:

"Everything must be arranged, and as soon as we hear the signal, we will attack.

Peter advanced followed by the patrol. The second lieutenant marched beside him in silence. The helmet and the submachine gun reminded Peter of his first fights in the Netherlands, when the war began.

They reached the other end of the lot. A soldier inadvertently kicked a can. In the silence of dawn it sounded like a cannon shot. Peter motioned for everyone to hide. Not far away, a voice asked in Polish:

"What was that, Sikorski?

"Nothing. It seems to me that you dream "they answered him.

Peter walked over to the fence and looked across. No one was there and nearby there was another alley that led to the track. The lieutenant colonel signaled and the patrol jumped out onto the street, heading toward the alley.

They walked through it in silence. With their weapons mounted, they stuck to the walls so as not to be surprised. They tried to tread cautiously so as not to attract the enemy's attention. They reached the end of the alley, distinguishing the road and, beyond that, the third shed of material.

Von Ritcher pointed to the building. There was no doubt that it was him. At the door was a sentry stuffed into a fur coat and with the holsters crossed over his chest.

The wall was in shadow and allowed them to get close to the train rails, but they had to crawl. They advanced, Peter marching first. As he reached the rails he raised his head. The building was not far away. His patrol, trained as it was, could catch up and overpower him before the rest of the partisans arrived.

He gestured to the sergeant and the sergeant took the hand pump, ripping the safety off. Then he threw it hard on the sentry.

At the same time, the lieutenant colonel shouted:

"Let's go guys.

The grenade exploded, knocking the sentry down, but the "hunters" were already running toward the building. The signal had been given and the entire assault battalion would attack to save their leader.

Two partisans came out of the booth and the sergeant slammed the machine pistol into their faces, knocking them down in a burst. They were already in front of the building. The second lieutenant threw himself on a window, at the same time that one of the soldiers struck with the butt of the rifle to open it. Peter, followed by the sergeant, entered the command post.

A weak electric light illuminated the room. Someone threw a chair, smashing it. But at that moment the window was opened, entering the milky light of dawn.

Peter faced the submachine gun and fired on two partisans who stood before him. Suddenly he saw a tall, strong man waving an automatic.

He grinned fiercely. This must be the SS Colonel. To make sure, he yelled:

Stychel.

Stanislas found himself discovered and stood up, preparing to fire. They had hunted him down and he didn't want to run away.

At that precise moment, Aleska left the next room. He watched the scene, realizing what was about to happen and hugged Stanislas, turning to the German officer. He had started to fire when the girl stepped between the two men.

The young woman's body shook, shaken by the steel whip. His pupils narrowed as his muscles loosened. The enemy officer lowered the machine pistol, staring at the scene in horror.

A raucous cry went up in the vicinity of the railroad track. The assault battalion attacked, preceded by tanks.

Given the attitude of the two leaders, the enemy troops gathered in that place did not shoot, looking at each other with surprise. The roar of battle could be heard. Then Captain Noraczewski grabbed the colonel by the arm, dragging him into the other room. He closed the door, preparing to flee through a window.

Stychel barely had the strength to move, but he followed his assistant. Everything had been so fast, it felt like dull. Throughout the line, the Polish forces were attacked by the Germans, who were pushing towards the railway station.

Major Wagner led his men expertly and skillfully. The tanks fired incessantly, opening gaps in the walls and knocking them down as they charged. The "hunters" on patrols, they were assaulting the enemy strongholds and dropping their hand bombs. Machine guns and machetes came into play, driving the Poles out of their redoubts.

Little by little, the forces were storming the buildings towards the railway station. But the SS colonel was safe and would return to the front of his men.

CHAPTER XVI

WHILE THE WAR CONTINUES

Noraczewski struggled with the colonel to remove him from the command post. Stanislas, still stunned, shouted:

"Aleska! Aleska!

The captain called another partisan, instructing him to help him take his superior away. Between the two of them they managed to dominate Stychel, who was struggling to return to the building. At last the partisan raised his pistol, landing a blow at the colonel's skull.

Fainted, they managed to remove him from there, while Major Dmowaki organized the defense against the desperate advance of the battalion of "hunters".

Once the lines were reestablished, although far from the station, which had been completely occupied by the Germans, the rebels managed to stop, after heavy losses and bloody clashes, the attack of the enemy battalion.

Stanislas regained consciousness, finding himself in an abandoned warehouse. Only Noraczewski accompanied him. The captain understood the state of mind of his boss and friend and did not want anyone to accompany him.

Stychel stared in a daze at the place where they stood, seemingly unable to remember what was happening. Suddenly his pupils lit up and he jumped to his feet.

"Aleska! Aleska!

Noraczewski approached, muttering:

Courage, Colonel.

Stychel lunged for the door, yelling:

"Why have you taken me away from his side? I want to rescue his body.

Noraczewski got in the way, explaining:

"You must think of your men, Colonel. Aleska will be buried by the Germans.

Stanislas lowered his head. He realized that, tortured by Aleska's death, he was about to forget the mission on his shoulders. It was necessary not to forget the hundreds of rebels who trusted him. He couldn't betray the cause he had given himself to.

But his misfortune wrapped him in invisible, though unbreakable, leggings. Aleska had died. It seemed impossible to him that this could happen. A few minutes before this enemy officer entered the command post, they had dined together, chatting and laughing. Even Noraczewski had taken part in the conversation.

Stychel's retina was still full of the image of the happy and happy girl. Only a certain melancholy in his gaze, which she tried to control, recalled the situation in which they found themselves. His laughter still seemed to him to feel a laughter free of worry and fear. He thought he still felt the perfume of her body.

And yet Aleska had died. He was no more than an inanimate corpse, his muscles torn and his laugh gone forever, that laugh that the colonel loved so much.

Desperate, he buried his face in his hands and gave vent to his grief, not ashamed of being seen by his assistant.

His anguish, when he realized that it was all over, that the dreams they drew together would never come true, completely overcame him and he burst into tears like a child.

Noraczewski watched him silently. He understood what that man must be suffering, before whose eyes and without his being able to prevent it, the woman he loved had died violently.

The colonel was oblivious to anything but his pain as the operation devised by General Bach-Zelewski began.

* * *

Fighting desperately to stop the Russian soldiers, news of the Warsaw uprising had spread throughout the front. For the Germans it represented an obstacle that prevented the arrival of food and ammunition trains.

The generals prepared their divisions to repel the Soviet attack, which they envisioned harder thereafter.

However, at the Russian headquarters ...

The military car, followed by a column of trucks and vehicles, advanced along the flooded road, while columns of infantry and tanks advanced through the field, next to the road. The artillery and cavalry continued their march, singing ancient songs.

A motorcyclist pulled up to the front car and saluted, handing out a sheet. Then he stood next to the entourage.

The man inside the car, a tall, muscular officer with white temples, opened the sheet, studying it carefully. That officer was Marshal Vatupin, chief of the Russian forces on the Polish border.

The marshal studied the letter and ordered the driver to stop. Then, while the cars of his entourage were imitating him, he approached a transmission truck and asked for a line with Moscow. He spoke on the phone for a moment and nodded.

The marshal paced for a few moments by the car, and turning to the assistant, ordered:

"Summon the army commanders.

Then he returned to the car, continuing the march. That night, as the insurgents fought desperately against Bach-Zelewski's attacks, the top leaders of the Russian army met.

Vatupin entered the isba where they had established their headquarters and looked at the uniforms, high and old-fashioned collars and riding breeches, with polished boots. Strange Russian decorations were lined on the men's chests.

"Generals" the marshal began to say, "we have received an order that we must comply with.

The officers raised their heads, regarding him curiously. Men were seen in the uniform of aviation, with that of the armored troops and with the fur caps of the Cossacks.

"This order is to stop us.

The news fell like a bomb at the military meeting. They all looked at each other in amazement. A tall, muscular general with slanted Mongolian eyes hastened to say:

"Stop now that we can maybe break through the front?

Vatupin nodded.

"They are superior orders, from whoever commands more than me. Furthermore, the Warsaw uprising must be let down before we continue. Then we will try to break the front again.

Immediately the precise orders were carried out and the Soviet troops stopped, grouping themselves in the most convenient positions and staying on the defensive, without attacking for a single moment the Germans, who were in a critical situation.

CHAPTER XVII

STUBBORNLY

"A part of our objective has been achieved" said Bach-Zelewski ", but we still need the most important thing.

The officers listened silently, waiting for him to continue their orders.

"We have only managed to capture the railway station, but not to expel the rebels from the Prague district. However, I must pay tribute to Lieutenant Colonel von Ritcher, who in an admirable stroke of audacity has achieved his first objective.

They all turned to Peter, who was standing still, his features drawn.

"I believe that the fight in that sector should continue until the rebels are crossed over the river or until they are isolated from the Alexander Bridge. But in the Nowe Miasto and Stare Miasto sector the banks of the Vistula need to be cleaned up. Both operations will be carried out at the same time, but with less intensity. The fight in Prague must continue as before, in successive blows that capture enemy groups and buildings turned into forts. On Nowe Miasto we will unleash an offensive.

That same afternoon, the streets near the river were filled with soldiers and tanks. Some accompanying artillery pieces had been set up in the intersections and on the corners, so that they were aimed at the rebel positions.

At a certain time they began shooting without rest. Buildings, turned into forts, jumped shattered, crushing their defenders. From time to time, the fire would cease and loudspeakers could be heard warning the rebels:

"Surrender. You cannot succeed and you will only achieve innocent victims. Surrender.

Then came artillery fire. But the Poles remained in their posts, ready to defend themselves.

At last, the enemy bombardment ceased and the assault tanks began their march on the opposing strongholds. Groups of soldiers, equipped with light weapons and flamethrowers, followed them, launching themselves on the partisan strongholds.

Automatic weapons began to rattle and hand grenades exploded as tank chains screeched and engines roared. The artillery of the armored monsters fired their salvoes on the buildings. The flamethrowers were spreading their waves of fire, opening the way for the troops and driving away the rebels.

Sapper Units they advanced with their dynamite charges, placing them in enemy redoubts to blow them up.

Little by little the waves of grenadiers and sappers, protected by the carts, made the rebels retreat towards the river.

Major H had secured reinforcements and the troops supporting him were sticking to the ground tenaciously. But he understood that if he did not manage to stop the German advance, he would be overwhelmed, leaving his men useless to continue the fight in the streets.

He went to the firing line, cheering on his troops. He went from one place to another, exposing himself constantly, but getting the men to show more enthusiasm.

The month of September had begun and the cold was beginning to spread throughout the city. Icy streaks came from the plain to the combatants.

Major H could make out the masses of tanks looming over the rubble, surrounded by the assault groups. Booms and bursts of automatic weapons made a roar around him, haunting and maddening.

He also saw how some combatants fled, terrified by the presence of tanks and flamethrowers, which were opening the way. A building from where several rebels defended themselves was taken by the sappers.

The German troops continued their way, irrepressible and overwhelming.

They had to be contained. He gave his orders and the volunteers flocked, establishing themselves before the enemy vanguards, which were charging furiously.

Among the rubble and among the ruins the partisans took cover, mounting their machine guns and mortars. They knew that if they isolated the tanks, annihilating the soldiers who accompanied them, it would be easier to fight them. But the flamethrowers and the hand grenades did not leave an instant of rest.

Major H understood that he would only achieve that his entire unit was annihilated and that not a single one would be able to continue fighting.

"It is necessary to resist until the night comes. Then we will cross the river again.

The explosions of the artillery mixed with the dynamite charges that blew the buildings. The clatter of machine guns indicated the advance, which was proceeding, slower but unstoppable.

Suddenly a shell exploded a short distance from the major, and he fell, bloodied. His last words were:

"Let them cross the river at dusk.

The fight continued with greater intensity. Despite the death of the leader, the Poles continued to fight with equal determination until night fell on the city.

Different boats had gathered at the river docks, and then the troops were embarking on the transports, marching towards the other shore.

Little by little the New City was abandoned and the partisans returned to the shore from which they started. They all felt enormous grief. It did not seem possible that everything could end that way, and they repeated:

"We will still be back.

However, their voices lacked the confidence of a few days before.

At last almost all of them reached the other shore, distinguishing from the barges how the German tanks and grenadiers reached the quay, from which they had fled.

Throughout that day, Colonel "Wladimir" managed to stop the advance of the armor on his lines. Through the wide avenues of the Modern Neighborhoods, the tanks advanced with ease, evolving without hindrance. But from neighboring houses and from half-demolished buildings they fired relentlessly at the troops following the carts.

They did not rest for a single minute. They continually raided homes, fighting room by room, until the partisans were driven out or annihilated. Flamethrowers relentlessly swept rooms and places where partisans resisted. Tanks were firing left and right, on neighboring buildings.

In the end, Colonel Wladimir had to retreat carefully without abandoning surveillance, to avoid being overwhelmed and succeeding in separating his troops from the bulk of the Clandestine Army.

They desperately left the Modern Quarter, heading towards the Old City. There they would resist until the arrival of the Russians or until Anders's army was landed from Italy.

On the outskirts of the city the prisoners captured by the Germans were gathering. The police troops guarded those men, in whose adventure they were abandoned.

Bor-Komorowski assembled his staff.

"We must make ourselves strong in the Stare Miasto, while we can. We will not leave an inch of ground more than when necessary. Let's wait for the arrival of the allies.

CHAPTER XVIII

ANNIHILATION

While in all sectors and neighborhoods outside the walls. The unstoppable pressure of the Germans continued, pushing the partisans towards the Stare Miasto, in the Prague district the battalion of "hunters" was preparing to annul the stronghold of the SS colonel's troops.

In the camp of the Germans, they strolled alongside the tanks and auto-machine guns, arms at arm's length. Cars equipped with antiaircraft machine guns also had to intervene in combat.

The railroad soldiers were working on fixing the tracks so that everything could keep running right away.

Suddenly the elegant figure of Lieutenant Colonel von Ritcher emerged from the command post. His face, despite retaining the usual serenity, was seen as contracted, and in his pupils a look of despair shone.

The soldiers looked at each other uneasily. They knew that since the assault on the enemy hut their boss was strange. They didn't ask why, but the news of a woman's death had circulated and perhaps this explained everything.

Von Ritcher, his helmet securely fastened and his submachine gun tucked under his arm, stared at his men. Everything was ready for combat.

He signaled and the vehicles advanced, fanning out toward the Alexander Bridge. Peter, accompanied by Captain Schulz, jumped into an auto-machine gun and set off, followed by the entire battalion. The fight began again.

The groups and the patrols advanced in pursuit of the armored cars, sweeping the enemy defenses. The auto-machine guns circulated, laden with "hunters," through the widest streets, leaping over rubble and over holes in the pavement made by artillery.

The cars armed with antiaircraft machine guns fired to zero, while the light detachments assaulted the opposing positions.

Stanislas received the news of the adversary advance. Still desperate for Aleska's death, which at times seemed impossible, he rose to his feet, cheering for the troops that were still waiting.

"We are going to stop them. And it's about von Ritcher, our enemy.

The partisans, arms drawn and frowning, went out to confront the enemy. The two opposing sides marched with the same decision and with their leaders at the fore.

The fighting began fiercely and continued harshly. German patrols leapt through the rubble, firing their machine pistol rounds and hand grenades at adversaries' nests and plunging bayonets into the enemy's body.

Tanks and armored cars fired incessantly, continually pressing toward the river. The red blazes of the flamethrowers rose from the buildings turned into battlefields.

Time and time again the "hunters" threw themselves on the adversary without resting. The corpses were lying in the rubble. The prisoners were pushed away from the fight, with their hands raised.

For once the partisans seemed to falter. A group of tanks wedged themselves, followed by the patrols, onto a wide street that allowed them to evolve.

Terrified, the Poles began a flight towards the Bridge, thinking of nothing else than to save themselves. Stanislas was warned of what was happening and ran to that place, accompanied by his assistant. He jumped out of the car, an elegant vehicle found in a garage, and exclaimed, addressing the fleeing partisans:

"Do you want them all crushed? Defend yourself, because if you don't, the tanks will scorch you.

The men, encouraged by his words, stopped, while he continued speaking and encouraging them to defend themselves. He saw a near ruined building at a short distance and pointed to it, adding:

"From there we can stop them.

The partisans took refuge among the ruins and among the rubble. The walls were half demolished, showing the holes made by artillery and dynamite charges.

From there they opened fire on the advancing chariots. The tanks stopped, keeping their fire on the enemy, while the infantry troops charged forward. The figure of an officer, elegantly dressed, was distinguished in the center. Stanislas thought he recognized her figure.

Little by little the German soldiers were advancing towards the building. Stanislas understood that it was necessary to resist or withdraw the troops to the other side of the Vistula, and while he remained in his post, he organized the withdrawal of other sectors.

At last the German "hunters" charged the building. They jumped over rubble and funnels, entering through gaps in the walls.

Stanislas took a submachine gun and began firing around him to defend himself. Suddenly he made out the figure of an officer leaping through a window, brandishing his submachine gun. He recognized him immediately. It was von Ritcher, the man who had killed Aleska. He faced the submachine gun and began firing on his enemy. The projectiles kicked up clouds of dust next to the officer, but missed him. Peter stood motionless, not firing, as the enemy fell back.

Evicted at the end of the building, the Poles retreated over the Alexander Bridge and by barge to the other shore. Peter was also in charge of that sector.

Once everyone was locked inside the Stare Miasto, General Bach-Zelewski initiated the siege. The cannons and tanks continued firing on the first houses on the other shore, while the troops prepared to launch their conquest. From time to time the loudspeakers repeated the well-known words:

"Surrender. You cannot succeed and you will only make useless victims.

Then Thor's mortar went into action. He began firing from his platform over the Old City. Their booms seemed to shake the entire city.

Little by little, the first streets of the Old City had been cleared of adversaries and the German troops set out to conquer them. They managed to land on the other shore and occupy the first houses. There they became strong and continued the march, through the narrow streets, amid a hail of bullets from unknown snipers who thus avenged their courage when they knew they had been defeated.

The fight continued. House by house, corner by corner, the Germans were conquering the Old City, while Thor's mortar unloaded its gigantic projectiles on the population.

Stychel kept looking for Peter in the fighting. He had reports that he always marched in front of his soldiers and that he guided them in the blows, but they never met again. The Pole said to himself that on only one occasion they had managed to see each other, and that he could not kill him, as was his wish. Aleska was still not avenged.

The cleaning operation continued, crushing the Poles who were still defending themselves close to the ground, they remained in their positions, protected by the narrow streets of the Stare Miasto.

CHAPTER XIX

BEFORE REALITY

The fight continued with intensity. The month of September had ended and the snow was already beginning to fall on the mountains. The cold air stretched over the burning city, yet not preventing the fighting from growing fierce.

The bombings and the fighting in the streets continued intensely. The grenadiers and the "hunters" were gradually invading the narrow streets of the Stare Miasto, receiving the shots of the snipers sheltered in the buildings.

That morning, October 1, 1943, General Bor-Komorowski met in the basement where he had his headquarters, with his assistants and the leaders of his army.

All showed the traces of the sustained struggle.

Several of them wore bandages and unhealed wounds. The desperate expression of men in the face of death could be seen on their faces, without the possibility of being saved. Tired, weary, nerves strained, they gathered there to decide the situation, in which they had hoped to succeed.

Stanislas, bitten by pain, stood at one end, staring at the ground. Dmowaki had died and Noraczewski had taken over the post. Many of his men had fallen in the cruel fighting, and their memories haunted the colonel.

The image of Aleska, lying on the ground, continued to haunt her.

Bor-Komorowski cleared his throat and stared at the men who had followed him in his desperate struggle.

"Gentlemen" he said ", I do not need to explain what is the situation in which we find ourselves. You, finding yourself in the middle of a fight, know it as well as I do. However, we have to decide what to do.

The assembled looked at him uneasily. Where was the general going to take them?

"Despite our initial successes, mainly due to the lack of outside aid, we find ourselves reduced to the Stare Miasto, which is continuously bombarded and swept away by the enemy. Our men fall or are captured. We are running out of food and ammunition. I think we only have one solution left. Surrender.

Among the officers there was a moment of surprise. Stychel could not contain himself and exclaimed, rising to his feet:

"Surrender? Was that what we threw so many men into the fight for? Are we not going to continue? We can still beat them and hold on.

Bor-Komorowski looked at him with some pity.

"Colonel, I know that you would give your life, and I would do the same, to keep our flag high. But keep in mind that we can no longer win and that it is our obligation to avoid all unnecessary victims. We have held our positions until it has been humanly impossible to move on. If any of you believe that there is some way to sustain yourself and continue until you have won, I am willing to listen to you. Otherwise, I will send a commission to General Schellenberg today.

No one dared to answer. Stychel covered his face with his hands. No, it was not possible for them to be defeated. They had to surrender again, as they did before, when they were invaded from two fronts at once. And yet he understood that the general was right. There was no other choice.

* * *

Stanislas gazed at the Alexander Bridge, over which a group of German uniforms was advancing, along with a white flag. He turned to the general's aides and said:

"They are coming.

Over that bridge, the young man reflected, General Bor-Komorowski's delegates were on their way to parley with the enemy, and it was through this very place that he had dreamed of leading his men to victory.

The Polish representatives met the Germans in the center of the bridge. Some wore their uniforms, covering themselves with military capes. The others wore their civilian clothes, stuffed into their coats. White flags waved above the two delegations.

On both sides, combatants on both sides watched what was happening, waiting for the result.

The head of the Polish delegation saluted with a nod.

"On behalf of General Bor-Komorowski, head of the Polish Army of the Interior, we come to negotiate the surrender of the troops.

The German officer asked:

"What conditions do you want?

"Above all, the general wants all his men to be considered as soldiers and not as snipers. He also wants the residents of Warsaw who have not taken part in the fight to be respected.

"I will inform my superiors of your wishes" replied the German.

Bor-Komorowski paced nervously around his office. It was the only time that this man bathed in serenity had lost his cool. Suddenly, one of his assistants entered the room.

"The Germans accept our conditions.

Komorowski passed his hands over his forehead, as if in deep relief, then turned to his assistants.

"I will go and sign the surrender at General Bach-Zelewski's office. He is the one who has defeated us.

He turned to his collaborators and said:

"I want you to let the rebels know that I congratulate them on their behavior. That each and every one of them have done their duty. They deserved better luck, but I have not been able to lead them to victory.

Then he held out his hand to his assistants. They shook the right hand of that calm and cold man. Then, followed only by an officer, he headed for the Alexander Bridge. Stychel, still speechless, watched him pass, head high, tucked into his coat and covering himself with a dark hat.

He advanced with a white flag to the other end of the bridge, where a German officer with a car was waiting for him. They climbed up to him, addressing the Komandatur. The general did not open his lips during the entire journey.

On reaching the Komandatur he jumped ashore and entered the office where Schellenberg and Bach-Zelewski were waiting for him. They both stood at attention, bowing their heads.

"I think the reason for my visit is very clear," he said in German. I wish to conclude as soon as possible.

Schellenberg showed him a letter written in German and Polish. Bor-Komorowski read it carefully and then signed it, without parting his lips.

"My assistant will give the order that the rebels surrender within an hour.

Bach-Zelewski then approached the other. Those two men, so different from each other, one fiery and audacious, the other cold and serene, looked at each other for a moment. At last, Bach-Zelewski said:

"General, just as I believed it my duty to fight you with all my enthusiasm, now, from soldier to soldier, I can tell you that I admire you and that I consider your men to be one of the best troops I have encountered.

Bor-Komorowski bowed, grateful from the bottom of his heart for the praise he gave his troops to the enemy general who had overthrown them.

CHAPTER XX

END OF AN ADVENTURE

At the agreed time, according to Bor-Komorowski's order transmitted by the assistant, the Polish Clandestine Army surrendered. Some, upon hearing the news, tried to flee, leaving Warsaw, to join the partisans who were still prowling the countryside, ready to continue sabotage and clandestine fighting. Of these, most achieved their objective, but some were captured by the Germans.

The rest, led by their leaders, surrendered and surrendered their weapons.

German patrols advanced through the alleys of the Stare Miasto, heading for the command posts of the sectors. The leaders waited for them silently and with contracted features. From time to time an isolated shot still rang out, but the vast majority of the partisans waited, arms at arm, for the moment of surrender.

The German patrols were spreading, while the rebellious troops surrendered, surrendering their weapons and forming an extensive column that headed towards the Komandatur area.

Silent, defeated, but not defeated, the partisans marched, guarded by the German police, towards the concentration areas, to be sent to the prison camps.

Von Ritcher's troops advanced over the Alexander Bridge to the command post of Colonel SS

Peter approached the house, half in ruins, and asked:

"Where is your boss?

Stychel came out of the hut, gazing at his adversary. His lips trembled for an instant, and then he replied:

"I am.

Peter and Stanislas stared at each other. Both appeared exhausted, both physically and morally. But the jaw of the victorious German was raised with pride, while the pupils of the Pole gazed at the other with hatred and fury.

"I await the surrender of your forces. I'm Lieutenant Colonel ...

"Von Ritcher" interrupted the other.

Peter nodded.

"Exactly, Colonel Stychel.

They looked at each other again, apparently unperturbed. Both knew that the other was not unaware of who his interlocutor was.

"You already know the clauses of the surrender signed by General Bor-Komorowski. I hope that you will comply with them.

Stanislas hesitated for a moment, as if he didn't know what to do. Then he turned to Noraczewski and ordered:

"Let the surrender begin.

Before the troops gathered there, the Poles advanced and surrendered their weapons. Then they met in groups, and as these were numerous, they were led to the other side of the river. Stanislas and Peter looked at each other in silence, not expecting either of them to speak.

Suddenly, a shot fired from a nearby window, knocking down a German soldier. The "hunters" threw their weapons at their faces, preparing to repel the action, while a few held their guns at the prisoners and the partisans who were surrendering. Peter stopped them with a gesture, indicating:

"Go find the one who shot. The others are not to blame.

A patrol went up to the building, while at a signal from von Ritcher the surrender followed. In the distance, isolated shots were still ringing out. German patrols advanced through the alleys with mounted weapons, occupying the positions abandoned by the partisans in the surrender.

At some points, thieves and thugs launched themselves on the ruined buildings, trusting in the mess that had formed at the time. German troops, aided at times by partisans, pursued and arrested the thugs.

At last the entire Stanislas column was disarmed and captured. In groups she was transferred to the other side of the river, to be admitted. Noraczewski and other officers had already laid down their weapons and were preparing to march. Only Stanislas was missing.

Peter turned to him, holding out his hand.

"Colonel" he said ", his weapons.

A flash of anger flashed in Stanislas's pupils and he raised his hand to his chest, drawing a pistol. He pulled the trigger, firing nose-to-nose at his rival. The projectile passed harmlessly past the young man. Peter lunged at the Pole, disarming him.

The "hunters" turned, looking for the author of the shot.

"It must be some sniper," said von Ritcher. Then he ordered Stanislas ": Come with me.

Alone, they entered the building. Stychel glared at the young military man and, unable to contain himself any longer, exclaimed:

"Why don't you kill me?

"I have concealed that it was you who had fired," said von Ritcher.

Stanislas clenched his jaws.

"Does he want to kill me with his bare hands?

Peter smiled bitterly.

"I would have already. You have given me reasons that justify me to my bosses. He has attacked me after the surrender.

Desperate, Stychel yelled:

"I don't want to owe you any favors!

Peter, unperturbed, asked:

"A few days ago you tried to kill me in combat. So I had an explanation. Why do you want to do it now?

Stanislas licked his lips.

"For the same reason. So it was not a coincidence, nor a chance of the war. I shot you knowing who you were, because I wanted to kill you.

Peter asked calmly:

"Do you want to tell me why?

Stychel looked at him for a moment, then said:

"You killed a girl. And I loved her.

Slowly, the German replied:

"I loved her too.

Stychel stirred furiously at the other.

"What does it mean?

"What you have heard. I loved her too, because she was my sister.

Stanislas stared at him in amazement.

"His sister? But if she was Swiss.

The other shook his head.

"No, Aleska von Ritcher was German like me. When the fight broke out it was offered to the Abwehr. I did not hear from her, except for a few letters, until I saw her in Warsaw some time ago. I never heard from anything else. Then I found out that she had been sent to locate the SS Colonel's command post so that we could capture him.

Stanislas stepped forward.

"Why do you injure your memory?

Peter shook his head regretfully.

"Injury his memory? But don't you realize what it means? She knew they were going to storm the command post and she stepped before you to serve as your shield. First he fulfilled his homeland and his duty. Then she complied with you, because she loved you too. I couldn't help it, it appeared when I had already pulled the trigger and I couldn't stop the blast. I realized in that moment. She wanted to die with you, if something happened to her.

Stanislas lowered his head. He was silent for a moment, then exclaimed:

"So everything is different.

Peter nodded.

"We have already buried her. I will be leaving for the Russian front shortly. I will go one last time to lay flowers on her grave. If you want, I'll do it for you too.

Stanislas nodded. Then he held out his hand to Peter, who shook it silently.

From the window, von Ritcher watched as Stychel joined a column of prisoners and walked away over the Alexander Bridge.

END